The Monster Fish

Written by Colin Thiele
Illustrated by Craig Smith

An easy-to-read SOLO
for beginning readers

SOLOS

Southwood Books Limited
4 Southwood Lawn Road
London N6 5SF

First published in Australia by Omnibus Books 1999

Published in the UK under licence from
Omnibus Books by
Southwood Books Limited, 2001

Reprinted 2001

Text copyright © Colin Thiele 1999
Illustrations copyright © Craig Smith 1999

Cover design by Lyn Mitchell

ISBN 1 903207 28 2

Printed in Hong Kong

A CIP catalogue record for this book is available
from the British Library

For Jeffery, who loves fishing – C.T.

For my seafaring mate, Phil – C.S.

Chapter 1

Ben lived by the sea. He loved fishing and often went out in the boat with his mum and dad.

Once a year the Big Boomer Fishing Contest was held. There was a prize for the person who caught the biggest fish on a hand line.

Ben was checking his fishing tackle for the contest when the phone rang. His mum answered it.

"Your cousin Andy is on his way," she told Ben. "He wants to come fishing with us."

Ben's dad rolled his eyes. "That boy is as clumsy as a puppy," he said. "He's sure to fall out of the boat."

"He'll be OK," Mum said. "He'll catch something."

Dad snorted. "The only thing he'll catch is a cold."

Chapter 2

The boat ramp was very busy on the day of the contest. A long line of boats waited to get in the water.

Andy's gear was a mess. It took him a long time to sort it out. While Ben helped Andy, Mum caught a sea trout and Dad caught a nice whiting.

At last Andy tossed out his line.

"Careful," Dad warned him. "That's where the reef is. You'll snag your line on the rocks."

9

Andy just smiled. He had already felt a tug on his line.

"I've caught something!" he shouted. "Something big!"

There was a storm of bubbles in the water and a big black shape came up on Andy's line.

It wasn't a fish.

It wasn't a lump of seaweed.

It wasn't an old boot.

It was a scuba diver. Andy had hooked her wetsuit.

She was *not* happy!

Dad looked at Andy. "I think we'd better move," he said.

Chapter 3

They pulled up the anchor and started the engine.

Andy stood up and waved good-bye to the scuba diver.

"Don't stand up in the boat,"
Dad shouted. "You'll fall – "

Too late. The boat rocked and Andy landed on his back with his legs in the air.

Dad shook his head. "At least you fell *into* the boat and not *out* of it," he said.

Chapter 4

At the next spot Ben and his mum caught three more fish. Dad caught a big squid.

Andy took a line from his fishing box. It was quite heavy, like thin rope.

"You could catch a whale with a line like that," Dad said with a smile.

Andy tied one end of the line to
the boat. On the other end he put
two big hooks and a huge bait.

Then he cast out and waited.

Suddenly the line hummed.

"I've caught a whopper!" yelled
Andy.

It was a huge snapper, nearly a
metre long. They could see its shape
on the end of the line.

When the snapper was alongside the boat it gave a flick with its tail and jumped right out of the water. It curved over and landed in the boat, where it flapped about madly.

"Look at that!" shouted Dad. "It's helped to catch itself! Have you ever seen anything like it?"

Chapter 5

The snapper was so big that it shook the boat.

"What a beauty!" Ben yelled.

"What a whopper!" Andy cried.

"It's a monster!" Mum agreed.

Everyone was laughing with joy. This fish would win the prize for sure!

Then the snapper gave another heave with its tail and flung itself into the air.

At the same moment something shot out of the sea like a rocket.

Huge jaws opened beside the boat.

The water boiled like an
exploding bomb.
The boat rocked wildly.
Ben cried out.

Chapter 6

It was a great white shark, longer than the boat. For a second Ben looked into its open jaws and saw its rows of terrible sharp teeth.

The teeth closed fiercely on the snapper, but as it tried to tear the fish away the shark was caught on Andy's big hooks.

It went wild. It rolled and plunged.
The sea was covered with foam.

The shark started to drag the boat forward. Ben and Andy screamed in terror.

"Cut the line! Cut the line!" Dad shouted. "If the shark dives, we'll be pulled under!"

Ben grabbed a knife and tried to slash the line, but he couldn't. The boat was heaving and rocking too wildly.

Suddenly the shark turned and charged at them. It bit the boat so hard that everyone was thrown to one side.

Dad was white with fright. "Hang on!" he yelled. "Hang on! Don't fall out!"

Chapter 7

At last the shark tore itself free and shot away.

Dad, Mum, Ben and Andy were left gasping and shaking, lying spread out on the bottom of the boat.

Ben was the first to move. He sat up and looked around. "Will it come back again?" he cried.

Mum shook her head. She was very pale. "I don't think so. It hated those hooks in its mouth."

"I think I've had enough fishing for one day," said Dad. "Does anyone mind if we go back now?"

Chapter 8

That was the end of it. They went back to the beach with wet tails.

A farmer won the prize with a salmon that only weighed five kilograms.

Ben and Andy couldn't believe it. "We caught a snapper ten times bigger than that," Andy said.

"*How* big was it?" the farmer asked.

Ben and Andy spread out their
arms. "It was *this* big."

"And I guess it jumped into your boat all by itself?" said the farmer with a grin.

Ben nodded. "Yes! And then it jumped out again, and a shark ate it."

"Do you expect me to believe that?" laughed the farmer.

Mum stepped forward. "It *was* a monster," she said. "And a shark *did* take it. Look ... I found these caught in the side of the boat."

She held out two huge white shark teeth.

"Wow!" said Ben.

Mum looked at Dad. "You thought Andy would only catch a cold, but he caught a monster fish," she said.

Andy sneezed. "Well," he said, "I think I caught a cold too."

Colin Thiele

When I lived in Port Lincoln, South Australia, I liked to go fishing. People said there were so many fish in the sea that if you sneezed they would jump into your boat straight away. That never happened to me.

I also saw great white sharks – some in the water and some after they had been caught. People took photos of the fishermen standing on the jetty beside their catch. Some of the sharks were four metres long and weighed more than a tonne. Their big sharp teeth would give you nightmares!

I remembered scenes like that when I wrote this story.

Craig Smith

Believe it or not, I've never gone fishing in my life!

I remember going to a fish market as a child and seeing all the different kinds of fish with their staring eyes. Some were hardly bigger than my finger. Others were very big, but not nearly as big as the snapper in this story.

Many people enjoy fishing, but I think it's more fun to go snorkelling along a reef. There is nothing quite like swimming among a large school of shimmering, darting, silvery fish. I would much rather look at them than catch them.

More Solos!

Dog Star
Janeen Brian and Ann James

The Best Pet
Penny Matthews and Beth Norling

Fuzz the Famous Fly
Emily Rodda and Tom Jellett

Cat Chocolate
Kate Darling and Mitch Vane

Green Fingers
Emily Rodda and Craig Smith

Gabby's Fair
Robin Klein and Michael Johnson

Watch Out William
Nette Hilton and Beth Norling

The Great Jimbo James
Phil Cummings and David Cox